The Kingdom of Wrenly

1
The Lost Stone

2
The Scarlet Dragon

3
Sea Monster!

By Jordan Quinn · Illustrated by Robert McPhillips

LITTLE SIMON

New York   London   Toronto   Sydney   New Delhi

LITTLE SIMON
An imprint of Simon & Schuster Children's Publishing Division
1230 Avenue of the Americas, New York, New York 10020
This Little Simon bind-up edition June 2017
The Lost Stone, *The Scarlet Dragon*, *Sea Monster!* copyright © 2014 by Simon & Schuster, Inc.
All rights reserved, including the right of reproduction in whole or in part in any form.
LITTLE SIMON is a registered trademark of Simon & Schuster, Inc., and associated colophon is a trademark of Simon & Schuster, Inc. For information about special discounts for bulk purchases, please contact Simon & Schuster Special Sales at 1-866-506-1949 or business@simonandschuster.com. The Simon & Schuster Speakers Bureau can bring authors to your live event. For more information or to book an event contact the Simon & Schuster Speakers Bureau at 1-866-248-3049 or visit our website at www.simonspeakers.com.
Designed by Laura Roode
Manufactured in the United States of America 0417 MTN
10 9 8 7 6 5 4 3 2 1
Library of Congress Control Number 2017934598
ISBN 978-1-5344-0934-7
ISBN 978-1-4424-9692-7 (*The Lost Stone* eBook)
ISBN 978-1-4424-9695-8 (*The Scarlet Dragon* eBook)
ISBN 978-1-4814-0074-9 (*Sea Monster!* eBook)
These titles were previously published individually in hardcover and paperback by Little Simon.

CONTENTS

The Kingdom of Wrenly

of

The Lost Stone

CONTENTS

CHAPTER 1

A Secret Mission

Prince Lucas raced up the spiral stone staircase in the castle to his bedroom. He kneeled on the floor and then pulled a pile of clothes out from under his bed. There was a pair of worn trousers, a shabby shirt, a felt hat, scruffy leather boots, and a wool cloak.

Lucas had gotten the clothes for a handful of coins from a boy in the village. Now the prince stood before a mirror and tried on the hat. *This outfit will make me look like a normal eight-year-old boy,* he thought. *Nobody will ever know that I'm the prince of Wrenly.*

And that was the problem. Lucas had grown bored of being a prince. Most kids would think, *He must be CRAZY!* Lucas had everything a boy or girl could wish for: a cozy goose-feather bed, toys fit for a prince, the best cooks in the land to make his meals, and a view of the sea from the top of his turret. Lucas even had his very own horse, named Ivan. But there was one thing the prince did not have. . . .

Friends. Lucas wanted a friend more than anything in the world.

He'd had a friend once—a pretty, green-eyed girl named Clara Gills. Clara's mother, Anna, made dresses for Lucas's mother, Queen Tasha. Anna always brought Clara when she came to the castle. Clara and Lucas had played hide-and-seek and twirled on the swings in the royal playroom. But not anymore. Lucas's father, King Caleb, had forbidden it. He had said a proper prince does not play with village children. Lucas had cried until his nose got stuffy.

So day after day Lucas watched the village children walk to and from school. Sometimes they stopped at the bakery for breadsticks. In the afternoons Lucas watched the children climb trees and play tag in the

meadows. How he longed to laugh
and play along with them!

And now maybe I can have friends,
he thought. *Because I, Prince Lucas,
have a magnificent plan!*

But Lucas had to hurry. It was

time to go. He stuffed the worn clothes into a sack and then slung the sack over his shoulder. Next he tied a thick rope to the windowsill, crawled onto the ledge, slid down the rope, and ran to the stables where he saddled Ivan. Then Lucas checked to see if anyone was around. *All clear,* he thought. He hopped onto Ivan, gave him a soft kick, and galloped away on his secret mission.

CHAPTER 2

Lucas the Brave

Lucas dashed over a bridge and down into the village. Chickens squawked and scattered to get out of his way. The villagers bowed and tipped their hats as he rode by.

Clang! Clang! The school bell rang down the lane. Lucas slapped the reins and hurried toward the sound of the bell. As he drew near, he leaped over a stone wall and came to a rest. He hopped from the saddle and quickly changed his clothes.

Lucas tucked his curly red hair inside the felt hat. Then he grabbed a handful of dirt and smudged his cheeks. He tied Ivan to a low tree branch, and hung the sack with his princely clothes from the saddle.

"Well, Ivan," he said, "here goes."

Lucas climbed over the stone wall and stood in front of the school-house. A swirl of smoke curled from the chimney. Lucas took a deep breath. *Today I am Lucas the Brave!* he said to himself. Then he marched up to the schoolhouse and slowly pulled open the doors. *Creak!*

The children sat in front of the teacher on benches. Everyone turned to stare at Lucas. A girl with a thin braid crowning her brown hair gasped and cupped her hand over her mouth.

"Good morning, boy," the teacher

said. "Are you here to join us?"

"Yes," said Lucas. "I'm new in town."

"Please have a seat," she said. "I'm Mistress Carson. What's your name?"

"My name is Flynn," fibbed the prince as he sat down on a bench at the back of the classroom.

"Welcome," Mistress Carson said. "Class, please say good morning to Flynn."

"Good morning, Flynn," said the class.

"Now all eyes on me," said the teacher. "We're going to work on subtraction."

The children turned toward the

teacher, all except the girl with the braided crown. It was Clara, Lucas's old friend from the palace. She looked at the prince and raised an eyebrow. The prince winked at her. She smiled and quickly looked away.

Nobody seemed to notice.

Mistress Carson wrote some sums on a large slate at the front of the classroom. "Now, who would like to solve a problem at the board?" she asked.

The prince's hand shot up. He loved to add and subtract. His father had taught him math at home. Mistress Carson called Lucas up to the board. The children watched as the new boy walked to the front of the class.

I'm going to have lots of friends!
Lucas thought. Then he began to
work on one of the problems. The
room was quiet, except for the chalk
tapping on the board, until . . .

Boom! Boom! Boom! Someone

began to pound on the doors of the school. The children jumped in their seats. Lucas froze. His heart began to thump. The teacher hurried to the back of the room and opened the doors. Two burly men burst in.

Lucas dropped his chalk on the floor. *Oh no!* he thought. *The palace guards!* He wanted to run, but the doors were blocked.

"There he is!" shouted one of the guards as he pointed at Lucas. "That's the prince of Wrenly!"

Mistress Carson and the children gasped.

The other guard ran toward the prince, grabbed him by the arm, and led him toward the doors.

Clara waved as Lucas walked by. Lucas hung his head.

Now I'll never have any friends, he thought.

CHAPTER 3

Kindness Is King

King Caleb threw Lucas's peasant clothes into the fireplace. They burst into flames.

"What were you thinking?" cried King Caleb. "You are a royal prince. You must behave like one. Peasants are not equal to royals."

"But, Father, I have no friends," said Lucas. "I'm bored out of my royal britches."

"You should spend more time with my knights," suggested the king. "You can train with them."

"It's not the same," said Lucas. "I'm lonely, and I need a friend my own age. I want somebody to talk to, and most of all, someone to go on adventures with me."

The king sighed. He hated to see his son so unhappy, but he couldn't allow him to be friends with the peasants. Even they would think it was strange. He looked to Lucas's mother, Queen Tasha, for help.

"Your father is right," said the

queen as she brushed her long red
hair. "But you are also right, Lucas.
You do need a friend."

She looked at her husband.

"Anna Gills is like family to
me," said Queen Tasha. "And her

daughter, Clara, was like a sister to Lucas. Perhaps we should allow them to play together once in a while."

King Caleb rubbed his blond beard thoughtfully. He was a mighty king, but he had a kind heart.

"All right then, Lucas," he said, "I suppose you may be friends with Clara. But you're not to make friends with every peasant child in the kingdom of Wrenly."

Prince Lucas ran to his father's arms.

"Thank you, Father," he said. "I promise."

CHAPTER 4

"Hear Ye! Hear Ye!"

Lucas couldn't wait for Clara and her mother to arrive at the palace. So he didn't. He snuck out and raced all the way to the bakery.

Clara always went to the bakery after school. Her father, Owen Gills, worked there.

Lucas peeked down the lane. *The school children are coming!* he thought. He didn't want them to see him, so

he pressed himself against the wall
alongside the bakery. Then he
listened to what they were saying.

"Why on earth would the prince
want to go to school with *us*?" asked
a boy named Albin.

"Maybe he's lonely," Clara said. "I

feel sorry for him, cooped up in the castle all day."

The children laughed at Clara.

"How can you feel sorry for the prince?" asked a girl named Sophia.

"The prince has everything!" said another girl, named Ashley.

"Not *everything*," said Clara. "He doesn't have a single friend. He's not even allowed to play with me when I visit the palace with my mother."

"Well, I'd trade places with him any day," said Albin. "I'd love to live like a prince."

"I know it sounds like the perfect life," said Clara, "but a palace, fine clothes, and delicious food aren't everything."

Bells jingled as the children stepped into the bakery. Moments later, each child carried a roll of

warm butternut bread to the bench outside. Lucas's mouth watered. How he wished he could join them! As he waited, he heard horses whinny. Then someone began to shout.

"Hear ye! Hear ye!" he cried. "The queen of Wrenly has lost her prized emerald stone! The king has offered a grand reward to anyone who finds it!"

The villagers began to hurry about to spread the news.

Oh no! thought Lucas. *I must get back to the palace!*

Lucas left his hiding place and ran all the way home, being care-ful to stay in the shadows.

A Royal Adventure

Queen Tasha sat at her dressing table, dabbing her eyes with a silk handkerchief. Lucas put his hand on his mother's shoulder. He knew the emerald meant a lot to her. It had belonged to her great-grandmother.

"Don't cry, Mother," he said. "I'm going to find your emerald."

His mother smiled weakly. Then she picked up the gold chain from which her stone no longer dangled.

"It could be anywhere," she said sadly. "I've been all over the king-dom these past two days.

"Where have you traveled to?" Lucas asked.

The queen thought for a moment. "I went to Primlox, Burth, and Hobsgrove," she said.

Lucas sighed.

"You're right. It could be any-where," he said. "But have no fear;

I'm going to find it. I'll need help though."

"What kind of help?" his mother asked.

"Clara's help," said Lucas.

The queen smiled and nodded. "All right," she said. "You have my permission."

"Thank you, Mother," said Lucas. "I *will* find your emerald."

Later that afternoon Clara and her mother arrived at the palace. Lucas grabbed Clara by the hand, and they raced to the royal playroom. Then he told her his idea.

"We'd search for the missing jewel together?" Clara asked.

"Exactly," replied Lucas.

"But will your parents allow it?" asked Clara with a frown.

"They already have after what happened today," said Lucas.

"What do you mean?" Clara asked.

"After I got caught at the school-house, my parents agreed to let us be friends again."

"You mean you didn't get into trouble?" questioned Clara.

"No," said Lucas. "I think they felt sorry for me."

"Why?"

"Because I have no friends," Lucas said.

Clara sat on the swing and looked at Lucas.

"Is it hard being a prince?" asked Clara.

"No, it's D-U-L-L being a prince," said Lucas. "And lonely. I can't even be friends with ordinary children."

"That royally stinks," said Clara.

Lucas laughed. "Well, at least *we* can be friends," he said.

"That's great news," Clara said. "So, when do we start our search?"

"Right now," said Lucas. "And our first adventure will be epic."

"I love epic adventures!" said Clara.

"Then let's make a plan," said Lucas.

Lucas laid out a map of the great kingdom. Then they marked all the places Queen Tasha had been over

the past two days. Clara knew the
kingdom of Wrenly well. She had
delivered bread to all the lands with
her father.

"I'll be your guide," Clara said.

"I can hardly wait," said Lucas.

"How about we meet outside the carriage house after breakfast."

"There's no school tomorrow so I'll be there," said Clara.

"Can I ask for a small favor?" said Lucas.

"Sure," Clara said.

"Will you bring some butternut bread from the bakery?"

Clara laughed. "Only if you bring me some yummy sausage from the royal pantry," she said.

"Deal," said Lucas.

CHAPTER 6

Rainbow Frost

Wrens, the small brown birds that gave the kingdom its name, twittered in the treetops as Lucas and Clara boarded a royal carriage. They would travel through Flatfrost and over the bridge to the island of Primlox. Lucas stuffed his map of the kingdom in his back pocket—just in case they needed it.

Four magical islands surrounded

the mainland of Wrenly. Primlox was ruled by the fairies. Hobsgrove was known as the island of wizards. The king's dragons roamed the island of Crestwood, and Burth belonged to the trolls.

All the islands were protected by the kingdom of Wrenly, but

each island was a smaller kingdom unto itself. King Caleb had to work very hard to keep the lands united. Sometimes there was trouble, but for now all was well.

As the carriage entered Primlox, Lucas and Clara saw the fairy queen, Sophie, floating before her castle. Queen Sophie had shimmer-ing gold wings and a rainbow-jeweled tiara. All the fairies wore clothes made from ferns, feathers, acorns, and flowers. Clara could tell they had used enchanted thread to sew their clothes, because all their outfits sparkled.

Thousands of smooth pebbles formed Queen Sophie's castle. The roof was shingled with shells, and the windows were made of sea glass buffed by the Cobalt Sea. The fairies fluttered toward the carriage.

"Welcome, Prince Lucas," said Queen Sophie.

"Thank you," said Lucas. "This is my friend, Clara. We've come in search of my mother's lost emerald. She said she visited Primlox just yesterday."

"I'm saddened to hear of her loss.

Follow us, and we'll help you retrace her steps."

Lucas and Clara followed the fairies along a path. They crossed over an arched bridge and into the Garden of Strawberries. All the fruit in the kingdom of Wrenly was grown in Primlox. But Primlox was also known for its sweet orange blossom honey.

In the middle of the Garden of Strawberries, Clara saw little round tables carved from tree stumps. Braided twig chairs and red-and-white-dotted stools made of mushrooms surrounded each table.

"Queen Tasha had mint tea and berries in the garden," Queen Sophie said. "She sat over there."

Clara and Lucas began to search for the emerald. They looked around the tables, under the chairs, and throughout the whole garden. But the only thing they found was a ladybug.

"Ladybugs are a sign of good luck,"

said Queen Sophie with a smile.

"We could use a little luck," said Lucas.

"Follow me," said Queen Sophie. "Your mother also strolled through the Maze of Hedges."

"What's the Maze of Hedges?" asked Clara.

"It's a maze formed by many rows of trimmed bushes," Queen Sophie explained.

Lucas and Clara stepped into the maze. They followed a path between the hedges. They couldn't see over the tops of the bushes, but that

didn't matter since they had to keep their eyes on the ground.

They zigzagged through the narrow dirt paths in search of the emerald. Sometimes the path led to a dead end. Then they had to turn around and go another way. Sophie and her ladies-in-waiting flew overhead to help guide them. They wound their way to a fountain at the center of the maze. There was no sign of the emerald. They searched the other part of the maze until they reached the exit. Still no emerald.

Lucas and Clara sat down on some mushroom stools to rest. Four fairies greeted them with a tray of lemonade. A small, nervous-looking fairy named Rainbow Frost fluttered up to Lucas and Clara.

"I may have a clue to finding the lost emerald," said the fairy in a high-pitched voice.

"What is it?" asked Sophie.

"I saw a lovely green stone in the Citrus Grove yesterday. I was going to pick it up, but my hands were sticky from collecting honey. I washed them in the fountain, but

when I returned, the stone was gone."

"Did my mother visit the grove?" asked Lucas.

"I'm afraid not," said Sophie. "But it's possible that a bird may have mistaken the stone for food and dropped it there."

"Oh no!" cried Clara. "That means another bird could have carried the stone anywhere."

"That's true," Rainbow Frost said. "But I'm not sure that's what happened."

"Why not?" asked Lucas.

"Because I saw a big troll in the citrus grove," Rainbow Frost said.

"And everyone knows trolls cannot resist treasure."

"Do you know his name?" Clara asked.

"His name is Hambone," the fairy said.

"We must leave for Burth at once!" declared Lucas.

"Let's go!" Clara said.

Queen Sophie loaned Lucas and Clara a boat to sail to Burth quickly. She also gave them a bundle of treats, which Clara tucked into her satchel. Lucas and Clara thanked the fairies and waved good-bye.

Hambone

Nobody greeted Lucas and Clara on the island of Burth. The trolls were neither friendly nor outgoing. They worked hard and grew vegetables for the entire kingdom. The kids walked to the stables in the village. Lucas tapped a sleeping troll on the shoulder.

The troll snorted and rubbed his eyes. "What do you want?" he grumbled, with one eye closed.

"We'd like to hire a horse," said Lucas.

"What for?" asked the troll.

"To visit a troll called Hambone," said Lucas. "Do you know where he lives?"

"Pay up," said the troll.

Lucas dropped a coin in the troll's grubby hand.

The troll smiled and bit the coin. "He lives on Old Tinder Road. His door is marked by the sign of a crescent moon," said the troll. "And don't tell him I sent you."

So Lucas and Clara mounted the horse and galloped along the rugged valley floor. Steep, craggy mountains towered over the island of Burth. The air smelled of garlic. They passed fields of corn, rows of turnips, and gardens of parsley. Soon the road began to go up. It twisted around and around a mountainside. Lucas and Clara passed cave dwellings all along the way.

"Whoa, back!" Clara cried as she jerked the reins. "We just passed a crescent moon!"

They tied the horse to a hitching post and knocked on the cave door

marked with the crescent moon. A
potbellied troll with green eyes and
wild gray hair answered the door.
He looked Lucas and Clara up and
down.

"We came for Queen Tasha's lost emerald," said Lucas. "Do you have it?"

The troll recognized the boy as the prince. He knew better than to play games with the son of the king.

"I found it in the Citrus Grove when I was gathering oranges," said Hambone.

Big grins spread across Lucas's and Clara's faces.

"But I no longer have it," he said gruffly. "I traded it for some hair-smoothing potion."

Lucas's smile disappeared. "So who has it now?"

"A wizard," said Hambone.

"Which one?" Lucas demanded.

"A wizard named Olaf," said the troll. "Now be off!"

And he shut the door with a thump.

"Looks like this adventure is far from over!" cried Lucas. "To Hobsgrove!"

Lucas and Clara raced back to the dock, boarded their ship, and sailed to Hobsgrove, the island of wizards.

CHAPTER 8

Olaf

The ship sailed past the island of Crestwood. Dragons played on the hillsides and soared overhead. Some snoozed in caves and some under the trees of the Great Pine Forest. A volcano puffed steam from the center of the island.

Soon the ship docked at Hobsgrove. A thick cloud of fog hung over the island. Even when

it was sunny everywhere else, Hobsgrove was always gray.

Ivy creeped up the dark walls and spires of the castle, where André and Grom, the two brothers who ruled Hobsgrove, lived. André was known to be very kind and friendly, but

Grom was not. He liked to keep to himself and spent most of his time in the dreary castle basement, mixing potions.

Many of the wizards on the island of Hobsgrove worked by the hearths of their thatched-roof homes. Their cauldrons bubbled with magical

healing potions made for the kingdom of Wrenly.

A young wizard brought Lucas

and Clara to Olaf's dark, smoky house. Olaf stood over his cauldron as it foamed and frothed. Lucas asked the black-bearded wizard if he had the missing emerald. The wizard shook his head glumly.

"No," he said. "That dreadful witch from Bogburp cursed me with clumsiness years ago."

"What does that have to do with the missing emerald?" asked Clara.

The wizard looked at them with sad brown eyes.

"The emerald fell from my hand after I returned home from Burth. It tumbled over Hob's Cliff and into the sea."

"Oh no!" Lucas cried. "That emerald belonged to my mother, Queen Tasha."

"That's most unfortunate," said the wizard. "Do tell her I'm sorry."

Lucas kicked a stone on the path as he and Clara headed back to the dock. "What are we going to do *now?*" he asked. "Go diving for it?"

"I have a better idea," said Clara. "Let's go to Mermaid's Cove."

"What for?"

"So we can leave a message in the sand for the mermaids," replied Clara.

"And how is *that* going to help?"

"Maybe the mermaids can find the emerald," she explained. "They always find the most beautiful shells and leave them on the beach for me."

"And how do you know it's the mermaids and not the tides?" Lucas asked.

"Because the shells are polished and perfect. None of them have been broken by the rocks and waves."

Lucas sighed and looked toward the mainland.

"It's worth a try," said Clara.

"I suppose," Lucas said.

So they boarded their ship and headed for Mermaid's Cove.

CHAPTER 9

Mermaid Magic

At Mermaid's Cove, the pink coral sand sparkled in the afternoon sun. Lucas and Clara kicked off their shoes and walked along the beach, looking for the perfect spot.

"Here's a good place," said Clara as she got down on her knees.

Lucas looked on as Clara wrote a message in the sand with a thin stick.

Dear mermaids,

Queen Tasha's emerald is lost in the sea off Hob's Cliff. Can you help us find it? Thank you for all the beautiful shells.

Love,

Your friend Clara

Lucas laughed. "You're crazy," he said.

Clara laughed. "I'm also hungry. Let's have our picnic."

Clara unwrapped the treats that the fairies had given them. Then she and Lucas sat by the far end of the cove. They talked and laughed and nibbled on bread, cheese, and grapes.

Lucas smiled at Clara. "I may

not have found my mother's emerald," he said, "but I have found one thing."

"What?" asked Clara.

"A real friend," Lucas said.

"Me too," said Clara. "I'm glad we can spend time together."

Lucas nodded. "We'd better get going. The sun's starting to set."

Lucas and Clara dipped their toes in the water as they walked down the beach.

"Look at your message," said Lucas. "It's already been washed away by the tide."

"Shall I write it again?" asked Clara.

"No, let's just head home," Lucas said. "We can come back tomorrow."

They sat on a rock to put on their shoes, but some shells caught Clara's attention. "Wow, these are beautiful," she said.

Lucas looked at a cluster of shells,

perfectly displayed on the sand.

"Were the shells here when we arrived?" he asked.

"No," said Clara. Her eyes grew wide. "The mermaids!"

"Mermaids again?" asked Lucas.

"I'm serious!" said Clara as she gently placed a shell in her satchel.

Clara loved to collect seashells.

"But we've been on the beach the whole time," said Lucas. "And we didn't see a single mermaid."

"Well," said Clara, "mermaids are very sly."

She picked up a half-open scallop shell and peeked inside.

"They're so sly that I've never ever seen one," said Lucas.

Clara handed the shell to Lucas.

"It's pretty," he said.

"Open it," said Clara.

Lucas opened the shell. He expected to see a clump of sand. But he saw something else.

"My mother's emerald!" he cried. "How could it be?"

"Mermaids," said Clara.

Lucas gazed out to sea. Then he looked at the emerald.

He couldn't believe it.

"Okay!" he shouted to the sea. "I believe!"

Lucas ran back to the shore and stooped to write in the sand.

Dear mermaids,

Thank you for finding my mother's emerald. Clara and I hope to meet you someday.

Your friends,

Prince Lucas and Clara Gills

Lucas put the emerald in his pocket. Clara placed the empty scallop shell in her satchel.

"For my collection," she said with a smile.

"I never would've found this without you," he said.

"What are friends for?" Clara asked.

Lucas smiled. "Race you to the palace!"

Then they quickly put on their shoes, and ran off.

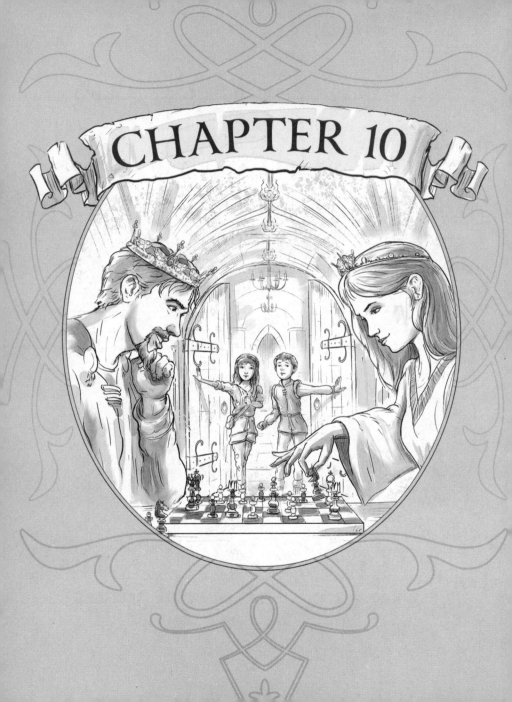

CHAPTER 10

Scallop

Lucas and Clara burst into the palace's great hall. King Caleb and Queen Tasha looked up from their chess game.

"What's all the fuss?" asked the startled king.

Lucas reached into his pocket and wrapped his fingers around the emerald.

"We have a very special present

for Mother," he said excitedly.

Lucas pulled his fist out of his pocket. Then he opened his hand to reveal the emerald.

Queen Tasha put her hand to her heart.

"Oh, you precious, brave, wonderful boy!" she exclaimed.

"It wasn't me, Mother," said Lucas. "Clara found it."

"We *both* did," Clara said.

"It was a real royal goose chase," Lucas added. "But Clara was the one who actually found it. She's very clever, Mother."

"Thank you, Clara," said the queen.

Clara curtsied.

King Caleb was very grateful. "You shall receive a handsome reward," he said. "Follow me."

Lucas, Clara, and Queen Tasha followed King Caleb through a heavy oak door and down a spiral stone staircase. They walked all the way to the royal stables. The king stopped in front of a stall. A beautiful brown horse with a black mane, black tail, white socks, and black hooves whinnied at them.

"Clara, this is your reward," said the king.

Clara gasped.

"You may ride her whenever you visit the palace."

"She's beautiful!" cried Clara as she pet the horse's mane. "Thank you, King Caleb."

"What would you like to call her?" asked the king.

Clara looked into the horse's eyes.

"I'd like to call her Scallop," she said. "Because we found the emerald in a scallop shell."

"A very good choice," said the king. Then he put his arms around Lucas and Clara. "I owe you two an apology. I'm sorry I didn't let you play together before."

"That's okay," Clara said.

"We know it's hard being a king," Lucas added.

The king and queen laughed. Then they went back to the palace.

Clara linked her arm with Lucas's. "Hey, friend—will you go riding with me?"

Lucas smiled. "I sure will."

The Kingdom
of
Wrenly

The Scarlet Dragon

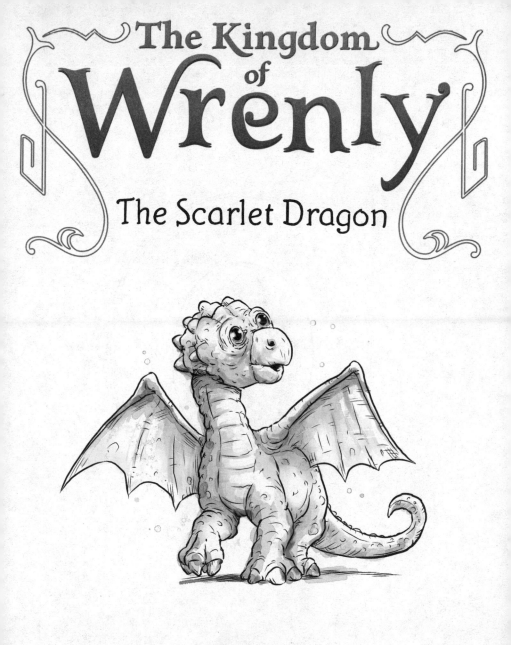

CONTENTS

CHAPTER 1

Red Alert!

Plump juicy sausages, fresh fruits, warm cinnamon rolls, and fluffy scrambled eggs sat on the table in front of Prince Lucas. The prince drummed his fingers on the white tablecloth and stared dreamily at a tapestry of a unicorn and a lion. He had hoped to meet up with his best friend, Clara Gills. But breakfast had gotten in the way.

"You have to eat something before you go," said his mother, Queen Tasha.

Lucas grabbed an apple from the fruit bowl and took a big bite.

"There," he said in between chomps. "*Now* may I go?"

"Please don't talk with your mouth full," said his father, King Caleb.

"And you must wait to be excused," said the queen.

Lucas sighed and took another bite of his apple. He could hear a pair of boots clip-clopping along the

stone floor toward the great hall. Stefan, one of the king's men, entered the room and bowed his head. The king and queen looked up from their breakfast. Lucas stopped munching his apple.

"Your Highness," said Stefan, "I have some very strange news."

"What can it be?" asked the king.

"André and Grom have found an orphaned dragon's egg on the island of Crestwood," Stefan said.

André and Grom were wizardly brothers and the rulers of Hobsgrove, an island province of the kingdom of Wrenly.

"Well, that's not terribly unusual," said the king.

"True, my lord," said Stefan. "But this dragon egg is *red!*"

Everyone gasped—including the servants.

"My goodness!" exclaimed the king. "Are you sure?"

"Yes, I saw the egg myself, Your Majesty," Stefan said. "It's a deep scarlet red."

"Whoa!" Lucas cried. "That means it's a scarlet dragon!"

Lucas knew that a dragon was always the same color as its egg.

"That's impossible," the king bellowed. "According to the legends, there hasn't been a red dragon in the kingdom for more than two hundred years!"

The great hall became quiet. Nobody dared to challenge the king.

Then King Caleb stood up. "I must see this egg at once," he said.

"Yes, Your Majesty," said Stefan. "I'll summon the royal ship."

"Father, may I go with you?" asked Lucas.

The king raised an eyebrow.

"Please?" Lucas begged.

"I'd like to go too," the queen chimed in.

Then the king laughed. "Okay, we shall all go," he said. "We'll leave for the dock in a few minutes."

"Yes!" Lucas shouted as he jumped up from the table. Then he quickly sat back down. "May I please be excused?" he asked.

"You may," said his parents.

Lucas bolted from his seat and raced all the way to the stables.

CHAPTER 2

A Fire Breather

Lucas spotted Clara outside a stall. He watched her gently brush her horse, Scallop. Scallop was a velvet-brown Arabian horse with a black mane, a black tail, and white socks. The horse had been a reward from King Caleb for finding Queen Tasha's lost emerald.

"Clara!" called Lucas. "You'll never guess what!"

Clara stopped brushing. Her green eyes lit up when she saw her friend.

"What?" she asked.

"André and Grom found a red dragon's egg on Crestwood!" said Lucas.

"A red dragon's egg!" exclaimed Clara. "Do you know what that means?"

"It means there's a scarlet dragon inside!"

"Exactly," said Clara. Then her face became serious. "And you know what they say about red dragons."

"Sure," answered Lucas. "The legends say they're the most magnificent dragons in all the world!"

"And the most feared," Clara added.

"Not to worry," Lucas said. "It's all in the training."

Clara rolled her eyes.

"Have you ever trained a fire-breathing dragon?" she asked.

"Actually, I've never even trained

a dog," Lucas said. "But the knights and wizards know all about dragon training."

"I suppose," said Clara. "But what if it sets Wrenly on fire?"

"Then we'll put the fire out," said Lucas. "Trust me. A red dragon is going to be amazing."

"Well, it certainly is exciting," Clara admitted.

Lucas gave Clara a pat on the shoulder.

"Well, I'd better be off," he said. "My parents are taking me to see the egg right now."

Clara waved as Lucas ran back to the castle.

CHAPTER 3

Eggshells

Lucas boarded the royal ship with his parents. It was a beautiful spring morning. The clouds had a reddish glow. *Maybe it's because there really WILL be a scarlet dragon in the kingdom of Wrenly,* he thought. Lucas grabbed the railing and looked toward Crestwood. He wished the ship would sail faster.

André met them at the dock.

"Come with me, Your Majesties," he said.

André showed the royal family to a waiting carriage.

"Where is the egg?" asked the king.

"Grom found it beside the lava flow."

"Are you sure the egg has been abandoned?" the king asked. He knew that mother dragons were very protective of their eggs.

"Yes," André said. "We've watched the egg for several hours, and there's been no sign of a mother."

"Why would the mother abandon her egg, anyway?" Lucas asked.

"Well, perhaps she feared the responsibility of raising a red dragon," André said. "One thing's for sure, she knew to keep the egg very warm."

"But I thought *all* eggs had to be kept warm," said Lucas.

"A scarlet dragon's egg must be kept near or over an open flame," André said. "I think she left the egg beside the lava on purpose."

"But these things are all based on legends," said the king. "Do you really believe in these stories?"

André looked thoughtful for a moment. "Well, we shall soon find out," he said.

The carriage bumped along the road. Soon they came to a clearing. Lucas could see the slow-moving lava. It oozed down the side of the volcano and into a creek that flowed into the sea. Steam rose from the creek where the lava met the water.

André parked the carriage and helped the king and

queen to the ground. Lucas jumped
to the dirt by himself.

"Over here!" shouted Grom as he
waved to the royal family.

André led the way to the dragon's egg. It sat nestled in a shallow hole next to the stream of lava. It was a deep scarlet red—just as Stefan had described.

The king kneeled beside the it. "It can't be . . . ," he whispered.

King Caleb began to inspect the egg. It was the size of a grapefruit. He looked at it from every angle. Then, with both hands, he gently lifted the egg to the light. Everyone could see the faint outline of the creature within. The king held the

egg to his ear and listened. Then
he carefully placed it back into the
hole. He looked at the two wizards
and his family.

"I never would've
thought it possible,"
said the king. "But this
is indeed a scarlet
dragon egg."

The queen clasped her hands together. "What an exciting thing to happen in the kingdom of Wrenly!" she exclaimed.

"I knew it!" declared Lucas. Then he grabbed his father's arm. "Can we take the dragon egg back to the palace?"

"No," the king said firmly. "The egg must remain in Crestwood until it hatches. It cannot be disturbed."

Lucas hung his head.

"But after the egg hatches," the king went on, "you may bring the baby dragon back to the palace."

"Will the baby dragon be mine?" asked Lucas.

"Yes," said the king. "I hereby proclaim the red dragon will be yours."

Lucas jumped into his father's arms and hugged him. "Thank you, Father! Thank you!"

"You are welcome, my son," the king said with a smile. "You must

take good care of your dragon. And with some help, you will learn to train him."

Then, with Lucas still attached, the king turned to Grom. "Will you continue to care for the egg until it hatches?"

Grom, who had raised many an orphaned dragon, knew exactly how to care for the egg.

"I would be honored, King Caleb," said Grom. "But I should like one thing in return."

The king raised an eyebrow. He

wasn't used to bargaining. No one would dare—except Grom. Grom was a slightly crafty wizard. He shared his great healing powers with the kingdom, but he could also be a troublemaker.

"And what would you like in return?" asked the king.

"I would like the scarlet eggshells after the dragon hatches," Grom said. Dragon eggshells were known to have magical powers. Grom was planning to use them in his potions.

"Very well," said the king. "I see no harm in it. You may have the shells."

Grom smiled crookedly. "Thank you, Your Majesty," he said.

CHAPTER 4

Nesting

News of the scarlet egg swept across the kingdom like dragon fire.

"It's a miracle!" some said. "A red dragon will surely bring good luck to the kingdom.

Others said, "Oh no! Scarlet dragons are bad luck. Nothing good can come from this."

The local merchants cashed in

on the news. An inn known as the Red Rooster had now become the Red Dragon. The grocer began to dye his eggs red. The village boys sold hand-carved red dragons by the side of the road.

But Prince Lucas had bigger things to think about. He had to design a lair for the scarlet dragon. Lucas and Clara learned everything they could about dragon lairs. They read books and talked to the knights and the wizards.

Then Lucas drew a plan for the dragon's home. The main entrance, which was behind the castle, looked like the opening to a cave. Rocks and boulders surrounded the mouth of the cave. Lucas added a ledge for the dragon to perch on. Underground tunnels formed

the inside. Each tunnel led to a
chamber. Lucas drew a sleeping
area, a dining space, and a playroom
with a wading pool and a waterfall.
He added a large fireplace to each
chamber, because he read
that red dragons
needed their homes
to be hot. Lastly,

he added an escape exit in case an enemy approached the lair.

Then Lucas presented his plan to his father. The king loved Lucas's ideas. He had his men draw up the official plan.

Meanwhile, Clara and Lucas planned to make chew toys for the baby dragon.

"I'll sew some stuffed animals," said Clara.

"I'll carve some wooden toys," Lucas said.

Over several weeks, Clara sewed and stuffed a rabbit, a bear, and a fox with her mother's fabric scraps. Lucas collected branches from the woods and carved a sea serpent, a boot, a war hammer, and some bones. When they were done, they

stored the chew
toys in a chest in
Lucas's playroom
until the lair was
finished.

The king's men
worked on the lair for
two months. While they were build-
ing, Lucas took dragon training
classes on Hobsgrove. André and
Grom taught him how to feed and
care for hatchlings. They also taught
him about dragon discipline. Lucas
shared everything he learned with
Clara. He wanted his best friend to

help him raise the dragon.

Then one afternoon a trumpet sounded. The king's men announced that the lair had been completed! It was time for the royal family and Clara to have the grand tour. The children brought the dragon's toys.

Everyone followed Stefan into the lair. Torches lit the tunnels. Even though it was a warm summer day, fires crackled in each of the chambers. This is the temperature it would have to be for the baby dragon. The king and queen walked around excitedly. They were very impressed.

"A job well done," said the king.

"A splendid dwelling," said the queen.

"Now all we need is the baby dragon!" exclaimed Lucas.

When they got to the playroom,

Lucas and Clara laid out the chew toys. While Stefan talked to the king and queen, the children dipped their feet in the wading pool. They left the lair through the escape exit, which led them to the west side of the castle, under the bridge.

The Hatchling

Stefan raced into the great hall.

"Hear ye! Hear ye! The time has come!" he shouted. "The dragon egg has begun to hatch!"

The royal family dropped everything they were doing and set sail for Crestwood. Again, André brought them to the dragon's egg. Sure enough, the egg had a crack that zigzagged across the middle.

"It won't be long," Grom said.

Everyone sat and waited. The egg lay very still. A hawk cried overhead. Quails rustled in the underbrush nearby. Wrens warbled in the treetops. Nobody said a word until the egg began to rock. It then wobbled and trembled. The egg rolled around, and then, all at once, the shell broke apart. And there in the center stood a very unsteady, very red baby dragon.

"*Aaack! Aaack!*" it cried, sticking out its red tongue.

The baby dragon was the size of

a kitten. It had the face of a lizard and horns on top of its head. It also had a long pointy tail, batlike wings, and two eyes that glowed like emeralds. The dragon was a stunning shade of crimson fire.

"It's extraordinary!" said André.

"It's adorable!" cried the queen.

"It's magnificent!" said Lucas.

"It's unbelievable!" said the king.

"It's a *boy*!" cried Grom, who swiftly swept the broken eggshells into a leather sack.

André lifted the dragon and let him perch on his arm. The hatchling

steadied himself with his wings.
André offered the dragon some
spinach and berries. But the
dragon didn't seem inter-
ested. He just wanted to
perch.

"May I hold him?"
Lucas asked.

André let the dragon
step onto Lucas's outstretched arm.
The dragon perched steadily.

"Lucas, you must take him to his
lair right away," said André. "Food,
home, and love are what the hatchling needs most now."

"*Aaack! Aaack!*" screeched the dragon.

Lucas gently pet the dragon's nubby horns. "Wow," he whispered. "My very own dragon."

CHAPTER 6

Redhead

Clara couldn't take her eyes off the baby dragon.

"He's beautiful," she said.

Even though they were in the lair, the dragon stayed on Lucas's arm.

"He thinks I'm his mother," said Lucas.

Clara laughed. "That's a good thing," she said. "Because you *are* his mother."

Lucas smiled. "Let's take him to the playroom and think of some names for him."

"I love to think up names!" Clara said.

They hurried down the tunnel to the lair's playroom. Lucas set the baby dragon on the floor. Then they

watched to see what he would do. The little dragon held out his wings and took a few quick steps.

"He is *so* sweet," Clara gushed. "Maybe we should call him Sweetie Pie."

"No way," said Lucas. "He needs a noble name."

They watched the baby dragon chase his tail. He went round and round. Then he noticed the chew toys and pounced on the rabbit. He batted it with his nose. Then he brought it to Lucas and dropped it on the floor.

"Good boy," Lucas said.

Clara smiled.

Then the dragon lay down in front of Lucas.

"Awwww," he said. "The little guy needs a rest."

Lucas pet the dragon's horns.

"Let's think up more names," Clara said.

"Okay," said Lucas. "How about Firefly?"

"I like it," said Clara. "What about Fireball?"

"That's a good one," Lucas said.

They thought of all kinds of names: Mr. Flame, Big Red, Bonfire, and Rusty.

"What do you think of Ruskin?" asked Lucas.

"I really like it," said Clara.

"It means 'redhead,'" Lucas said.

"Even better!" said Clara.

"Okay! Then his name shall be Ruskin!" Lucas declared.

Then he addressed the baby dragon. "Hello, Master Ruskin," he said.

The dragon didn't respond.

"That's okay," Clara said. "He doesn't know his name yet."

Lucas tried again—a little bit louder this time. "Hey, Ruskin!"

Ruskin didn't react at all.

"Maybe he's hungry," Clara said.

Lucas offered the dragon some olives and rhubarb. Ruskin didn't even sniff the food.

"Maybe he's thirsty," said Clara.

They carried Ruskin to the

wading pool. He just lay in a heap beside the water and didn't move.

"Uh-oh," said Lucas. "Something's wrong."

"You're right," said Clara. "He doesn't look well."

"We'd better get help," said Lucas.

"You go," said Clara. "I'll stay here."

Lucas ran as fast as he could to the castle.

CHAPTER 7

Vixberries

The king summoned André and Grom to help the sick dragon. The wizards brought herbs, magic stones, and charms to the lair. They mixed garlic, red nettle, and raspberry tea. Grom laid a circle of magic stones around the dragon. Then Grom opened Ruskin's mouth while André spoon-fed the potion. They rubbed ointment on the dragon's scales and

waved charms around his head. The wizards even gave him an herb bath. But Ruskin was still limp, and his eyelids drooped.

André stood before Lucas and the king.

"I'm afraid the hatchling is very

ill," he said. "I've seen this before. The illness comes on fast and rarely ends well."

"André, you have to help him," Lucas pleaded. "I don't want to lose him!"

"Nor do I," said the king.

André looked grim. "There's only one known cure," he said.

"What is it?" they asked.

"A combination of mint tea and vixberries," André said. "The trouble

is, vixberries were once plentiful in the kingdom. But now they're almost impossible to find."

"Nothing's too hard for the king's men," said the king. "I'll order a search party. Where shall I send them?"

"The Starless Forest on the island of Burth," said André. "The place where vixberries grow is said to be

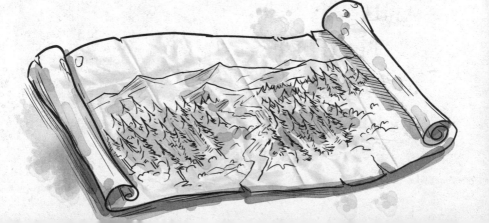

enchanted. It's been a secret for generations, and no one knows just where they are."

"My men will scour the forest," said the king. "I will reward whoever finds the vixberries with twenty pieces of gold."

"If Ruskin is to live, we'll need the berries by sundown," said André.

"But that gives us only one after-noon!" cried Lucas.

"That's not enough time!"

Lucas's eyes filled with tears.

King Caleb wrapped his arms

around his son and held him close.

"We have to have hope," said the king. Then he took off to organize the search party.

Clara put her hands on Lucas's shoulders.

"It'll be okay, Lucas," she said. "I have an idea."

Lucas wiped his eyes with the backs of his hands. "You do?" he said.

"Yes," she whispered. "But we have to leave at once."

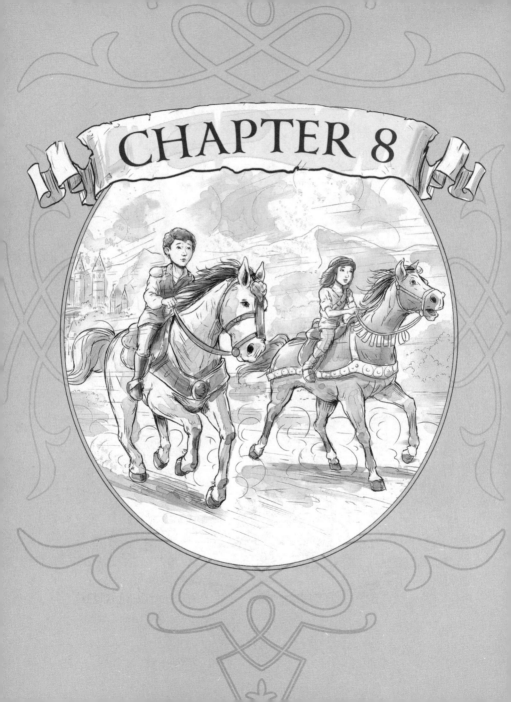

CHAPTER 8

Bren

Clara grabbed Lucas by the hand, and the two of them ran to the stables. After saddling Scallop and Lucas's horse, Ivan, they hopped on and galloped over the bridge to Burth.

"Where are we going?" shouted Lucas.

"You'll see!"

Clara and Lucas thundered along

a dirt road until they came to a stone cottage surrounded by orange lilies. Clara and Lucas tied Scallop and Ivan to a hitching post. Then Clara pounded on the door.

A short, stocky troll with rosy cheeks and sparkling blue eyes answered the door.

"Well, hello, Clara!" the young troll exclaimed. "Why the heavy hand? Are you delivering bread with your father today?"

Clara shook her head. "No, Bren," she said. "The prince and I have come to ask for your help. The scarlet dragon is very sick. He needs vixberries before sundown or he'll die."

The troll's expression became very serious.

"What makes you think I know anything about vixberries?" asked Bren.

"Because you told me about them one time, and nobody knows the Starless Forest better than you," said Clara. "Can you help us?"

Clara had known Bren ever since she could remember. They were the same age and often played together when her father delivered bread to his customers on Burth. Bren had shared magical stories about the Starless Forest.

Bren sighed as he thought about what Clara had just asked.

"The king has promised a generous reward," said Clara.

"Oh?" questioned Bren. "What kind of reward?"

"Twenty pieces of gold," Lucas replied. He knew that all trolls loved gold.

Bren looked around to see if anyone else was listening.

"Okay," said Bren. "I will get you vixberries."

Lucas and Clara clapped their hands.

"May we go with you?" asked Clara.

"No," Bren said. "The location is a secret. I'm the only one who knows. My father told me about it before he passed away."

"*Please?*" begged Clara.

"No way," said Bren.

"What if something happens to you?" asked Lucas.

"Then no one will ever know where the vixberries are," added Clara.

Bren knew this was true. He also knew he was going to have to tell

someone about the vixberries someday. He was almost certain Clara
and Lucas could be trusted.

"Perhaps you are right," he said.
"But you must promise never to tell
a soul."

"We promise," said Lucas and
Clara.

"Okay," said Bren. "Then we must leave right away if we hope to find the vixberries before sundown."

Bren gathered torches, water, and some leather pouches. He slung a wool bag with a long strap across his chest. Then he placed a worn felt hat on top of his head.

"Let's go," he said.

The Breach

The children hiked through a field of cornstalks, which grew from the land that the trolls had farmed for hundreds of years. Lucas and Clara carefully followed Bren over a swaying rope bridge and into the Starless Forest. As they tramped along, Lucas told Bren about the baby dragon. The woods grew darker and darker. Soon it became too dark to see. Bren

lit a torch for each of them.
After a while he stopped
and put a hand to his ear. "Do
you hear that?" he asked.

Lucas and Clara stood still
and listened.

"It sounds like rushing water," Clara said.

"It's the Lost River," said Bren. "Follow me."

Lucas and Clara stayed close to Bren. Soon he stopped again, this time beside two enormous boulders. Bren reached into his wool bag and grabbed a handful of dried lavender petals. He sprinkled them over the boulders. The boulders began to rumble. Then an opening appeared.

Clara and Lucas gasped.

"What's going on?" Clara asked.

"This is the Breach," said Bren.

"What's that?" asked Lucas.

"It's an opening in the forest," said Bren. "It's the only place in the Starless Forest where the sun shines."

"But why?" asked Lucas.

"Long ago, a wizard enchanted

the place to protect the unicorns from being hunted."

"You mean unicorns really exist?" Lucas asked.

"Yes," said Bren. "But today only in the Breach."

"Wow," said Clara. "No wonder it's a secret."

"And a very sacred one," Bren said. "It's now the only place where the vixberries grow too. Follow me."

They climbed through the opening in the rocks. A tunnel twisted

and turned before them. As they walked, the sound of the water grew louder. Then they turned a corner, and suddenly the tunnel was filled with sunlight.

Lucas and Clara shaded their eyes with their hands. From the cave opening they could see a waterfall tumbling into a pool of sparkling water. A mother unicorn and her colt drank at the water's edge. Wrens twittered. The ground was covered with forget-me-nots: tiny sky-blue flowers with a white inner ring and a yellow center. Butterflies

flitted above the flowers.

"Wow. This is paradise," Lucas whispered.

"It's magical," said Clara.

"Come on," Bren said. "We'd better hurry."

They snuffed the torches and left them in the cave. Then they walked over to the water.

"Over there," Bren said.

He pointed to some thorny vines that had climbed the rocks beside the stream. Plump white berries dotted the vines.

"Those are vixberries," said Bren.

He handed a pouch to Lucas and one to Clara.

The kids scrambled toward the

vines and plucked the white berries.

Plop! Plop! Plop! They filled their leather pouches. When they were done, they lit their torches and retraced their steps through the tunnel and out of the forest. By the time the kids got back to Bren's cottage, the sun had already begun to go down.

"You must go," said Bren.

Lucas and Clara thanked their friend and promised not to say a word about the Breach.

"You'll get your reward," Lucas said.

Bren nodded. "Hurry," he said. "I hope it's not too late."

Lucas and Clara hopped back onto their horses and raced over the bridge and up the hill to the lair.

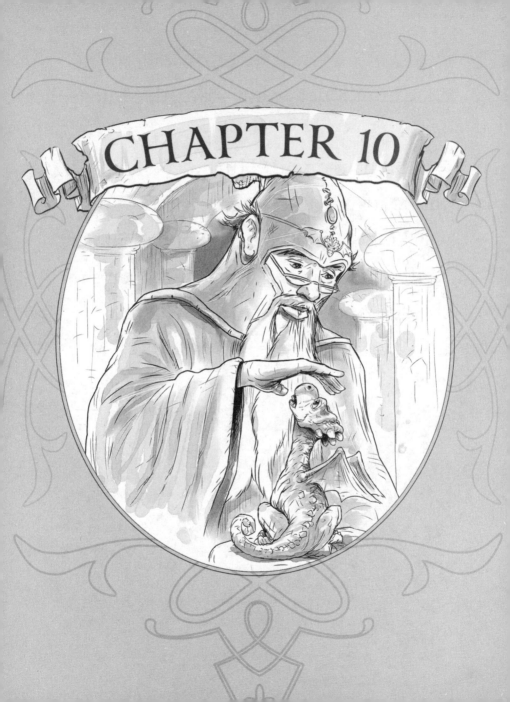

CHAPTER 10

Wake Up!

"Is Ruskin alive?" shouted Lucas as he entered the lair.

"Shhhh—don't startle him," said André, stroking Ruskin's head. "He's alive, but he's very, very sick."

"Here," said Lucas, handing André the pouches. "Clara and I brought you something."

"What's this?" asked André as he loosened the strings on one

of the pouches and peeked inside. "Vixberries!" he exclaimed.

There was no time for questions. The wizards went right to work. André poured the berries into

a mortar and crushed them with a pestle. Grom brewed some mint tea. As soon as it boiled, he poured it over the crushed berries. Then André stirred the mixture until it was blended. Grom opened Ruskin's mouth, and André fed the dragon a spoonful of the potion.

"Now what?" asked Clara.

"Now we wait," said André.

They sat and watched the baby

dragon. Ruskin just lay there. Grom checked Ruskin's pulse.

"Is he still alive?" asked Lucas.

"He's fallen asleep," said Grom. "Perhaps you and Clara should get some rest too," André suggested.

"No way," said Lucas. "I'm staying right here until he wakes up."

"Me too!" said Clara.

"Very well," said André.

Then André went to the palace. He told the king to call off the search party and gave him the latest news. When André returned, he brought  a loaf of bread and a large pot of wild rice soup with some bowls. Stefan followed with pillows and blankets.

"King Caleb will

allow you to stay," André said to the children.

They all ate supper as they watched over Ruskin. Grom set a plate of food in front of the dragon. Every few minutes Lucas checked to see if Ruskin was still breathing. Then, sometime before dawn, everyone fell fast asleep.

And that's exactly when Ruskin
woke up.

"*Aaack! Aaack!*" he squawked.

Lucas opened his eyes to find the
baby dragon sitting by his side and
looking into his eyes. The plate of
food beside Ruskin was empty.

"Ruskin!" he cried. "You're all better!"

Ruskin squawked again.

And it was true; Ruskin was well. The next day the king and queen threw a dragon baby shower for the whole kingdom. Bren got his reward, and Lucas and Clara honored their promise to keep the Breach a secret.

And from that day forward, Ruskin began to grow. He also learned how to fly! Now the only thing Ruskin needed was training. Lots of training.

But that's another story.

The Kingdom of Wrenly

Sea Monster!

CONTENTS

CHAPTER 1

Go Fetch!

Prince Lucas tossed a dinner roll across the royal kitchen. Ruskin, Lucas's pet scarlet dragon, scampered across the stone floor and gobbled the roll in one bite.

"Good boy!" Lucas shouted.

Ruskin ran back to Lucas, eager to fetch another snack. Lucas always sneaked treats for Ruskin when the kitchen servants were on their

afternoon break. He reached for a
leftover apple fritter this time.

"The more you eat, the bigger
you'll get!" said Lucas.

He couldn't wait for Ruskin to
grow big enough to carry him and
his best friend, Clara. They dreamed
of going on high-flying adventures.

Ruskin yelped for his snack. Lucas threw the apple fritter across the kitchen. The fritter landed next to the hearth. Ruskin zoomed after it, paying no attention to the cast-iron pots and pans stacked neatly beside the hearth. *Crash!* The pots and pans toppled over and clattered across the stone floor.

"What on earth is going on?" bellowed King Caleb, who had just entered the room.

"Oh, not much," said Lucas. "Just getting Ruskin a little snack."

Ruskin burped and a little puff of smoke came out. Lucas waved the smoke away and tried not to laugh.

"Isn't he great?" asked Lucas.

The king raised an eyebrow and polished an apple on his purple velvet robe.

"Tell that to the royal cook," the king said. "Ruskin scorched ten dish towels this week."

Lucas patted Ruskin's swept-back horns.

"He didn't mean any harm," said Lucas.

"Nevertheless," said the king, "he'll need better manners if he's going to come inside the castle."

Lucas had been training Ruskin to be a good dragon. The problem was that Ruskin didn't know how to control his fire-breathing. Sometimes he had accidents, and sometimes he scorched things for fun. Lucas was trying to teach Ruskin to use his fire-breathing skills for good causes, like lighting the hearth or roasting marshmallows.

"Don't worry, Father," said Lucas. "Soon Ruskin will be the most well-behaved dragon in all of Wrenly."

"Well, that's the best news I've heard all day," said the king as he left the room, munching his apple.

CHAPTER 2

A Creature
from the Sea

Lucas and Ruskin played one more game of fetch the snack. Then Lucas stuffed an apple fritter into his pocket for later. The two playmates skipped past King Caleb on their way outside. The king sat on his throne and stared out to sea.

Lucas turned around.

"Is something wrong, Father?" Lucas asked.

The king scrunched his brow and sighed.

"Perhaps," he said. "We've had some troubling reports from the fishermen."

"About what?" asked Lucas.

"Giant waves in and around the Sea of Wrenly," the king said.

"Must be a storm brewing," Lucas said.

"That's my guess," said the king, "but some say they've seen a large creature in the water."

"What kind of creature?" asked Lucas, becoming more interested.

"Something big," the king said. "Like a whale or a giant octopus."

"Or maybe a sea monster!" said Lucas.

The king raised an eyebrow. "That's ridiculous!" he said. "There are no such things as sea monsters."

Ruskin squawked.

"That's not what I've heard," Lucas said. "My old nursemaid, Nanny Louisa, told me a story about a sea monster. She said she saw it with her own eyes."

The king chuckled. "I know that story too," he said. "The legend of the

Great Sea Serpent has been around for years."

"It has?" questioned Lucas.

The king nodded.

"But how do you know it's not true?"

"Because it's not," said the king. "And I certainly don't want my people to worry about something that doesn't exist."

Ruskin let out a long, low howl.

Lucas and the king looked at the young dragon.

"Good heavens," commented the king. "What do you suppose he is trying to say?"

"I don't know," said Lucas. "Maybe that he believes in sea serpents."

CHAPTER 3

An Old Wives' Tale

"Well, I believe in sea monsters too!" said Lucas. "And I have a plan."

Ruskin scampered after Lucas. They ran all the way to Ruskin's lair. Once they were inside, Lucas played a trick on Ruskin. He reached into his pocket, pulled out the apple fritter, and tossed it deep into the cave. Ruskin ran after it. Then Lucas turned around and ran back out

the entrance. He slid the heavy oak
door across the opening and locked
Ruskin inside. Ruskin whimpered.

"Sorry, boy," Lucas said. "But this
plan doesn't include you. It may get
dangerous."

Ruskin squawked loudly.

"Someday, when you're bigger and stronger, you can come with me," said Lucas. "But not this time."

Lucas raced back to the castle and into the chambers belonging to his mother, Queen Tasha. He opened the door and bumped into Anna Gills. A few bolts of fabric fell from

her arms. Anna was the royal seamstress. She was also Clara's mother.

"I'm so sorry, ma'am," said Lucas
as he helped pick up the fabric.

"What's the hurry, Lucas?" asked
Anna.

"Forgive me for rushing," said
Lucas. "I'm looking for Clara. Do
you know where I can find her?"

Anna smiled.

"Clara is at Mermaid's Cove, collecting seashells," she said.

Lucas thanked Anna and zoomed off. He jumped from rock to rock as he bounded down the path to the beach. Something scrabbled over the rocks behind him. Lucas stopped and turned around. He didn't see anything. *I thought I heard something behind me,* he wondered to himself. *I guess I must have kicked a rock.*

Lucas continued down the path. He spotted Clara sitting on a large rock. Her brown hair was partly up in a braided crown. She held a string of shells in her hand. An old net lay on the rock behind her.

"What's that?" asked Lucas, stopping in the sand in front of Clara.

"It's an old fishing net," Clara said. "It washed up on the beach today. It's perfect for stringing shells."

Clara held out a necklace. It had

slipper shells, moon shells, and angel wings.

"It's beautiful," said Lucas as he hopped up and sat on the rock beside his friend. "So, you'll never guess what!"

"What?" asked Clara.

"There's a monster lurking in the Sea of Wrenly," Lucas said.

Clara's eyes widened. "What makes you say that?" she asked.

"My father says some of the

fishermen have seen a huge creature in the water. I'm pretty sure it's the Great Sea Serpent."

Clara laughed. "That's silly. Everyone knows that the sea serpent story is just an old wives' tale."

"I'm not so sure," said Lucas.

"Do you actually believe in sea monsters?"

"Yes, I really do," said Lucas. "My old nursemaid, Nanny Louisa, told me she saw the Great Sea Serpent with her own eyes."

"She did?" questioned Clara.

Lucas nodded. "And she would never make up something like that," he added.

"I never dreamed that story could be true," said Clara. "What do you think we should do?"

"Let's talk to Nanny Louisa," said Lucas. "Maybe she can help."

"Where does she live?" asked Clara.

"On the island of Primlox," said Lucas. "She's now a nurse to the fairies."

Clara slipped her shell necklace into her leather pouch. "What are we waiting for?" she asked. "Let's go!"

CHAPTER 4

Nanny Louisa

Lucas and Clara ran to the royal stables to saddle their horses, Ivan and Scallop.

Lucas lifted a saddle from the wooden saddle rack. Something in the window above him caught his attention. He climbed onto the saddle rack and peeked outside.

"What are you looking at?" Clara asked.

"I saw something in the window," Lucas said. "But now there's nothing out there."

"Maybe it was a bird," said Clara.

Lucas shrugged. "Maybe," he said.

Lucas and Clara placed a saddle onto each horse and tightened the straps. Then they set off for Primlox.

As they galloped past Flatfrost, Lucas noticed whitecaps on the water up ahead. *Wow, the sea monster really is making the water choppy,* Lucas thought.

When they got near the bridge,
they pulled back on their reins.
Villagers rushed back and forth
across the bridge.

"The bridge sure is busy," Clara
said.

"We'll have to walk the horses
over it," said Lucas.

They led Ivan and Scallop over
the bridge and tied them to a post
on the other side. The harbormaster

stood nearby, ringing his hands.

"What's wrong?" Lucas asked.

"It's been a very bad day, Prince Lucas," said the harbormaster. "The sea is too rough for travelers." He walked up closer and leaned in toward Lucas. "And there have been

rumors of something in the ocean."

Lucas and Clara gave each other a knowing glance.

"Well, we've come to see Nanny Louisa," said Lucas. "Do you know where she might be?"

The harbormaster nodded. "She's

tending to Fairy Queen Sophie. The queen has a very bad cold."

Lucas and Clara thanked him and headed for the fairy castle, a beautiful palace made of polished pebbles, shells, and sea glass. The fairies-in-waiting led them up the curvy stone staircase to Queen Sophie's chambers.

"*Ah-choo!*" The queen sneezed as the guests entered the room.

A puff of sparkly fairy dust flew from Queen Sophie's nose and mouth. She was sitting in her canopy bed, wearing a pink silk nightgown with enchanted milkweed fluff around the neck.

Nanny Louisa sat in a rocking chair beside Queen Sophie's bed. She handed her a handkerchief. Then Nanny Louisa stood up and greeted their guests. "Well, if it isn't my

chubby little bunny and his friend!"

Lucas blushed and Clara giggled. Lucas had been a very chubby baby, and Nanny Louisa always brought it up. She held out her jiggly arms and gave Lucas a great big hug. Then she looked at Clara.

"I remember you," said Nanny Louisa. "You deliver bread with your father. And your mother is Queen Tasha's seamstress."

Clara recognized Nanny Louisa too. She had a round, dwarflike body

and long white hair. Her eyes were kind and her smile was wide. Lucas formally introduced the two.

"Please excuse my stuffy nose," said Queen Sophie. "Tell me: What brings you to the palace?"

Nanny Louisa pulled up two chairs, and Lucas and Clara sat down.

"We have some questions for Nanny Louisa," said Lucas.

"We also wondered if you've heard the rumors," Clara said.

"What rumors?" asked Nanny Louisa.

Queen Sophie sat up in bed. "Yes, what rumors?" she asked.

"The Sea of Wrenly has been unusually rough," Lucas said, "and some say they've seen a big creature in the water."

Nanny Louisa's eyes grew wide, and she placed one hand over her mouth. "Oh no," she whispered. "The Great Sea Serpent."

Lucas nodded.

"You're joking, right?" questioned Queen Sophie.

But nobody laughed.

"Tell us, Nanny Louisa," said Lucas. "Is the sea serpent real—or not?"

Nanny Louisa sank into her rocking chair and sighed. "Most believe the sea serpent to be a myth," she said. "But those who have seen the great beast feel differently."

"We would love to hear your story, Nanny Louisa," said Clara.

"Yes, please tell it!" begged Lucas.

Nanny Louisa shut her eyes and told the story from long ago.

CHAPTER 5

Once in a Blue Moon

"I remember the day well," Nanny Louisa began. "I was a young maiden in those days—not a single gray hair nor a wrinkle. I worked at the Dew Drop Inn. I often served a young gentleman known as Captain Douglas Brown. Captain Brown was strong, kind, and well-liked in the village. One rainy night he asked me to be the cook aboard his ship, the

Blue Moon. He planned to take some men on a fishing trip. I have always liked adventure, so I agreed to go.

"We sailed the open sea for three weeks. The boys caught mackerel, tuna, and herring. Then we set our course for home. I stood on deck and

enjoyed a gentle breeze. I watched the clouds turn pink. Then my eyes fell on a dark patch of water. *A patch of seaweed,* I thought to myself. I looked more closely and noticed the dark water begin to boil and churn. *A pod of dolphins?* I wondered.

"Then something unimaginable happened. A creature began to rise from the water. It rose higher and higher—above and beyond the mast of the *Blue Moon*. It had the head of a dragon, with two horns and a mouth full of daggerlike teeth. The creature had a never-ending neck of green scales for a body, like an enormous snake.

"But the strangest thing of all was the rusty old cauldron that hung from the monster's jaw. It looked like a wizard's cauldron, though cracked and broken. *Why*

does it have a cauldron in its mouth?
I wondered.

"I stared—too scared to move.
A brave sailor grabbed a spyglass
and climbed the rigging to the
crow's nest to get a better look.
Others began to throw things at the
creature: boat hooks, silverware, and

dishes—anything that might scare it away. The monster roared and threw his head to one side. Then it flung the cauldron right at our ship!

"The cauldron crashed onto the deck, and we dove to get out of its path. The ship rocked this way and that. Captain Brown quickly spun the wheel to get us to safety. Then the men pulled themselves up and threw more things at the monster."

Nanny Louisa shut her eyes and rocked in the chair as she remembered the story.

"Please go on, Nanny Louisa!" cried Lucas.

"Oh yes!" exclaimed Clara. "Tell us what happened next!"

Nanny Louisa opened her eyes and continued her story.

CHAPTER 6

A Message

"'Wait! Leave the beast alone!' Captain Brown shouted.

"The fishermen stopped striking the sea monster. The serpent roared and plunged beneath the water. Enormous waves rocked our ship. Green seawater splashed over the deck. *We're done for!* I thought as I landed on top of my shipmates. Somehow I dragged myself to my feet and looked out on the water.

"The sea serpent slithered away. Loop after loop of its scaly green body curled through the water as it went on its way. None of us spoke.

We looked at the cauldron, which had left a large hole in the deck. *Had the monster been trying to tell us something?* we wondered. Perhaps the monster didn't like that garbage was being thrown into its watery home. We all agreed that the people of Wrenly needed to change their ways.

"Captain Brown took us to port.

We told King Henry—King Caleb's
father—what we had seen and
heard. The king believed every word
of our story. He knew he could trust
Captain Brown.

"'But you must never speak of it,'
said the king. 'We mustn't upset the

good people of Wrenly.' He also said that if we didn't have evidence of a monster, then no one would believe our tale. Then King Henry made a royal decree:

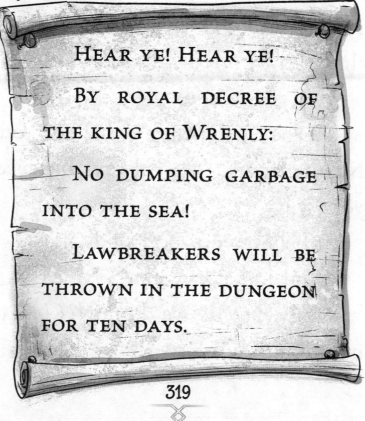

HEAR YE! HEAR YE!

BY ROYAL DECREE OF THE KING OF WRENLY:

NO DUMPING GARBAGE INTO THE SEA!

LAWBREAKERS WILL BE THROWN IN THE DUNGEON FOR TEN DAYS.

"Some of the fishermen told the story of the sea serpent against the king's wishes. But no one believed them. The villagers made fun of the fishermen and called them crazy. But I'm here to say—cross my heart— that every word of this story is true."

Everyone sat in silence.

Then Lucas said, "I believe you, Nanny Louisa. I've always believed you."

"I believe you too," said Clara.

"And I," said Queen Sophie.

"But what do we do now?" Lucas asked.

CHAPTER 7

Captain Brown

"Here's what you must do," said Nanny Louisa as she gave a doll-size spoonful of a potion to Queen Sophie. "You must find out what's bothering the sea serpent."

"But how?" asked Clara.

"There's only one way," said Nanny Louisa. "You must find the sea serpent and let him tell you."

Lucas and Clara looked at each

other and gulped. But Nanny Louisa was right. How else could they find out what was bothering the sea serpent?

"We're up to the task!" said Lucas and Clara together.

"Will you come with us, Nanny Louisa?" asked Clara.

"No," said Nanny Louisa. "I must stay with Queen Sophie until she feels better."

Queen Sophie had fallen asleep while they were talking.

"Then we'll be on our way," Lucas said. "Thank you for everything, Nanny Louisa."

Nanny Louisa hugged Lucas and Clara. "Be careful," she said.

"We will," promised Lucas.

Lucas and Clara hurried down the hill to the water. Empty ships bobbed up and down at the dock. Lucas tapped the harbormaster on the shoulder.

"We need a ship," Lucas said.

The harbormaster turned and faced Lucas and Clara.

"I'm sorry, Prince Lucas," he said. "But the captains have all gone home for the day. Nobody wants to

set sail in this rough water."

"But we're here on official royal business," said Lucas in his most grown-up voice. "We need to search for the sea monster."

The harbormaster stroked his chin thoughtfully. He knew better than to argue with royalty.

"Excuse me," said a scruffy-looking man who had been listening in. "May I be of some help?"

The man had a toothless smile, like a jack-o'-lantern's. He wore a tattered brown coat and old trousers. His knotted gray beard matched his straggly gray hair. He face was weathered, and he had friendly blue eyes.

"Who are you?" Lucas asked.

"I'm Captain Brown," said the man.

Clara and Lucas gasped.

"*The* Captain Douglas Brown?" asked Lucas.

"At your service," said the captain.

"But how did you find us?" asked Clara.

"A special friend sent for me," said Captain Brown. "She said it was urgent."

"Nanny Louisa!" cried Lucas.

"Aye. She may have had a bit of a part in it," the captain said.

"I'm not sure I like the idea of the

prince and a young maiden hunting for sea monsters," interrupted the harbormaster.

"Come," said Captain Brown, ignoring the harbormaster. "My ship, the *Blue Moon*, awaits. Have you any payment?"

Lucas and Clara looked at each
other. They didn't have a single
shilling. Then Clara reached into
her pocket and pulled out her shell
necklace.

Captain Brown smiled. "That will do nicely," he said. "Let's go find ourselves a sea monster."

Then they followed the toothless, bearded captain to his ship.

FLOUR

CHAPTER 8

An Old Friend

The ship pulled away from the dock and suddenly leaned to the right. Lucas and Clara held on to the side of the ship to keep from tumbling into the water.

"How are we going to find the sea monster?" asked Clara.

"Don't worry," said Captain Brown. "The sea serpent is going to find *us*."

"What could be bothering him?" Lucas asked.

"We shall soon find out," said the captain.

Sailing around the mainland, they passed Hobsgrove, Crestwood, and Burth. Saltwater sprayed as they

rode up and down the waves. Lucas
thought he saw something flicker in
the crow's nest. He looked
closely but didn't see
anything. *My eyes
must be playing
tricks on me,* he
thought.

When Primlox
came back into view, they had seen
no sign of the sea monster.

"Where is that old beast?" the
captain shouted over the wind.

"Let's go around again!" yelled
Lucas.

"It's too rough!" said Captain Brown. "We'll try again tomorrow."

"Please!" begged Lucas. "Just one more time around!"

Before Captain Brown could answer, the ship began to rock violently.

The ocean rumbled like thunder. The water churned and boiled, like a bubbling broth.

"Hold on!" Captain Brown shouted.

Clara and Lucas clutched the side of the ship with all their strength.

"What's happening?" Lucas cried.

"It's my old friend!" shouted Captain Brown as he pointed to the water up ahead. "The sea monster!"

Lucas and Clara saw the beast rise out of the water. They both screamed. It had the head of a fearsome dragon and a neck that stretched on forever—just as Nanny Louisa had described! Its green scales shimmered in the gray afternoon light.

The ship
jerked violently this
way and that. Lucas lost his grip
and tumbled across the deck.
He managed to grab hold of a rope
to keep from falling into the water.
When he looked up, the sea monster towered over the ship. It roared.
Then it lunged right at them.

Captain Brown spun the wheel away from the sea monster, but the captain lost control of the boat. Seawater flooded the deck.

"Hang on!" the captain cried.

CHAPTER 9

A Swirl of Fire

Somehow the ship stayed afloat. But the sea monster roared with fury. *It's going to swallow us whole!* Lucas thought. He squeezed his eyes shut.

"Lucas, open your eyes!" shouted Clara. "I see something caught on the sea monster's head!"

"She's right!" Captain Brown shouted.

Lucas opened his eyes and looked.

He hadn't seen it before, but the sea monster had a net stuck on its head.

"How can we free it?" asked Clara.

"We need to get closer!" shouted Lucas.

"Too dangerous!" cried Captain Brown.

Squawk! cried something from the crow's nest.

"What was that?" shouted Lucas.

"Up there!" yelled Clara.

A streak of red flew from the crow's nest.

"It's Ruskin!" Lucas yelled.

Ruskin squawked again and flew onto the sea monster's head. The sea monster tried to shake him off. But

Ruskin clung on to him.

"What's he doing?" Captain Brown shouted.

"I think he's trying to free the sea monster!" said Lucas.

Ruskin pulled at the net on the sea monster's head. He tugged and tugged, but the net wouldn't come free. Suddenly, Ruskin roared, and a little swirl of flame burned away some of the netting. Then Ruskin easily removed the rest of the net and flew a short distance away.

The sea monster shook its head. Its face became calm, and it sank

back into the sea. The water stopped churning, and the boat stopped jerking this way and that. Ruskin flew back to the ship and landed on the deck. He dropped the net at Lucas's feet.

Clara leaned over and picked it up.

"It's an old fishing net!" she exclaimed. "Just like the ones I use

to string my shell necklaces."

"The fishermen must be toss-
ing their old nets into the sea," said
Lucas. "And this one got tangled
around the sea monster's head."

"No wonder the sea monster was
mad!" said Captain Brown.

"Wow," said Clara. "If it hadn't been for Ruskin, the sea monster would have sunk our ship."

"Good boy, Ruskin," said Lucas, patting him on the back. "You used your fire to do something good!"

Ruskin rubbed his head against Lucas's legs.

"How do you think Ruskin found us?" asked Clara.

"I'm not sure," Lucas said. "I must've left the escape exit open, and then he was able to follow us by flying high above."

"Your dragon saved the day," Captain Brown said as he steered the ship toward Primlox.

Ruskin squawked.

"He sure did," Lucas said.

CHAPTER 10

A Royal Decree

The ship docked at Primlox, and Lucas and Clara said good-bye to their new friend, Captain Brown. They unhitched Ivan and Scallop and galloped back to the palace. Ruskin flew close behind.

The sun had gone down by the time they reached the stables. The stable hand began to feed and water their horses. Lucas and Clara thanked him and raced to the great hall with Ruskin at their heels. The king, the queen, and Anna jumped up from the table when the children walked in.

"Where on earth have you been?" demanded King Caleb.

"We were so worried!" said Queen Tasha.

"Just look at you two!" said Anna.

Lucas and Clara looked like they'd been washed in with the tide. Their clothes were soaked, and they had seaweed tangled in their hair.

"We went looking for the sea monster," said Lucas.

The king raised his hands and looked at the ceiling. "And did you find one?" he asked.

Lucas and Clara looked at each other and grinned. Then they shared their adventure.

"And Ruskin freed the sea monster with a little swirl of fire," finished Lucas.

Clara pulled the fishing net from her pouch and placed it on the table. The queen and Anna looked it over.

"Quite a remarkable tale," said the king. "You two certainly have wild imaginations."

Then Queen Tasha put a hand on the king's shoulder. "I'm not sure they're making it up," she said. "Look at this."

Caught in the net was a shimmering green scale. The king untangled it and looked at it closely. He turned it over and rubbed it between his fingers.

"Well, look at that," said the king.

"*Now* do you believe us?" asked Lucas.

"Yes," said the king. "I'm afraid I do."

Lucas folded his arms. "There's one thing I don't get."

"What's that?" asked the king.

"How come people get scared when they hear rumors of a sea serpent? And then, if someone actually finds one, they don't believe it?"

"Well," said the king, "sometimes you have to see something in order to believe it."

"Like you?" Lucas asked.

"Yes," said the king. "Like me."

"Are you going to tell the people of Wrenly that the sea serpent is real?" asked Lucas.

"Yes," said the king as he laid the scale on the table. "Since we have proof, I will tell the people, and I will also make a new decree. I shall call it the Rule of the Great Sea Serpent.

From now on, no fishing nets shall be thrown into the Sea of Wrenly. They must be mended or thrown away properly. Lawbreakers will be sent to the dungeon for ten days."

Then Lucas made his own royal decree. "Hear ye! Hear ye!" he said in loud voice. "I hereby proclaim that I am as hungry as a sea monster!"

"Me too!" Clara chimed in.

Everyone sat at

the table—except for Ruskin, who sat on the floor beside Lucas's chair— and had a dinner of pork roast, vegetables, and Ruskin's favorite: apple fritters. Ruskin ate five apple fritters and burped. A little ball of fire slipped out and charred the tablecloth.

Everyone laughed—even the king.

Enter

The Kingdom of Wrenly

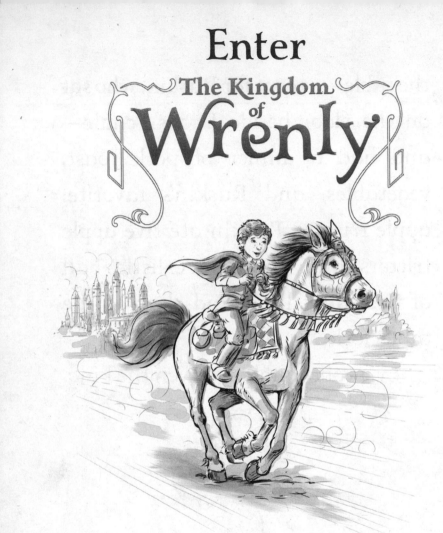

For more books, excerpts,
and activities, visit
KingdomofWrenly.com!